# THIS BOOK BELONGS TO:

_____

# THIS BOOK IS DEDICATED TO ALL THE ENGINEERS AND FUTURE ENGINEERS.

Copyright © 2024 Grow Grit Press LLC. All rights reserved. No part of this book may be reproduced in any form without permission in writing from the publisher. Please send bulk order requests to info@ninjalifehacks.tv

Paperback ISBN: 978-1-63731-939-0
Hardcover ISBN: 978-1-63731-941-3
eBook ISBN: 978-1-63731-940-6

Printed and bound in the USA.
NinjaLifeHacks.tv

Ninja Life Hacks®
by Mary Nhin

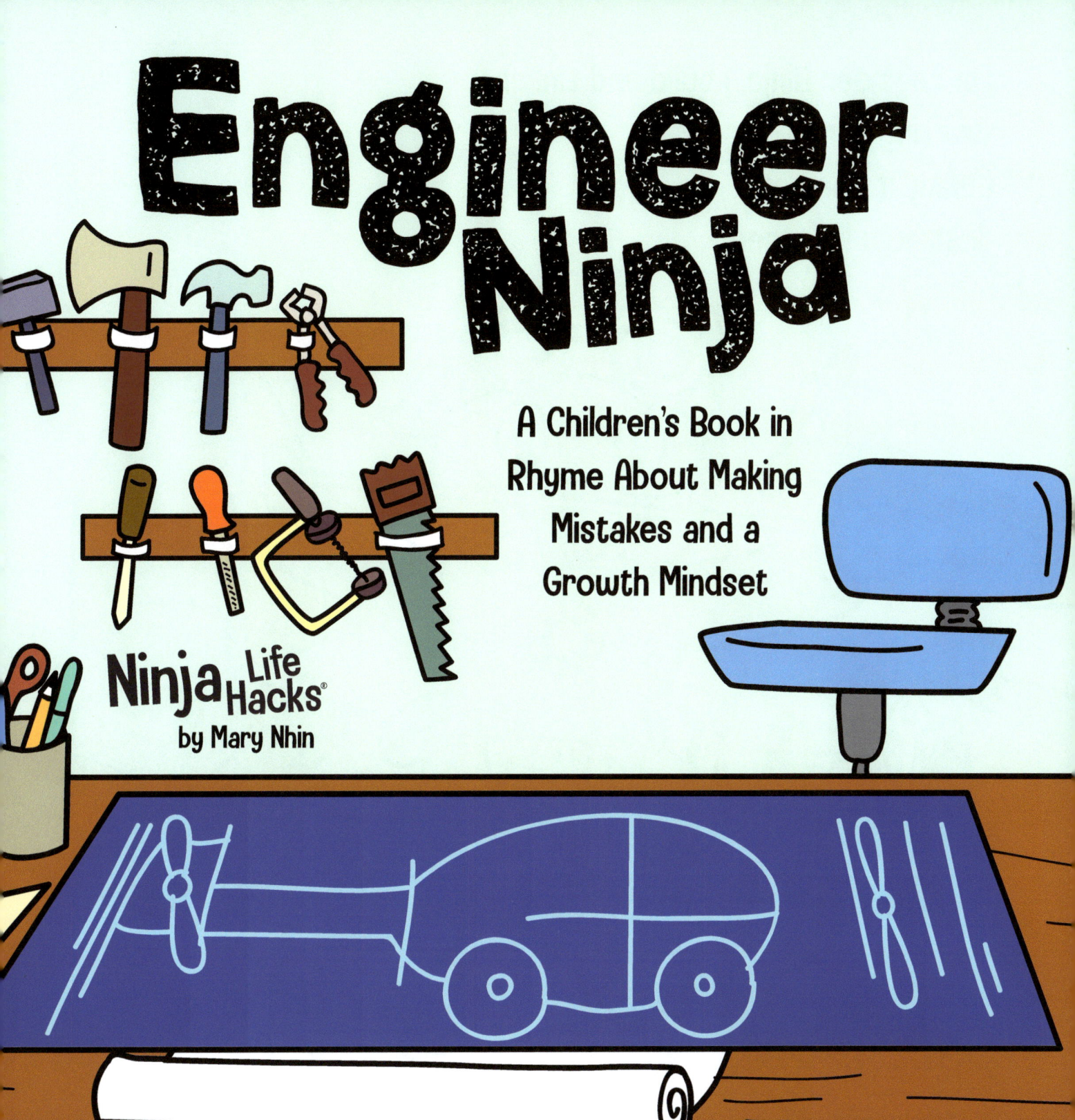

Today, I designed a machine
Built to fly,
With bolts and gears
To reach the sky.

I wanted to cry,
And give up the fight,
But my friends said,
"Engineer Ninja, it's okay if it's not right."

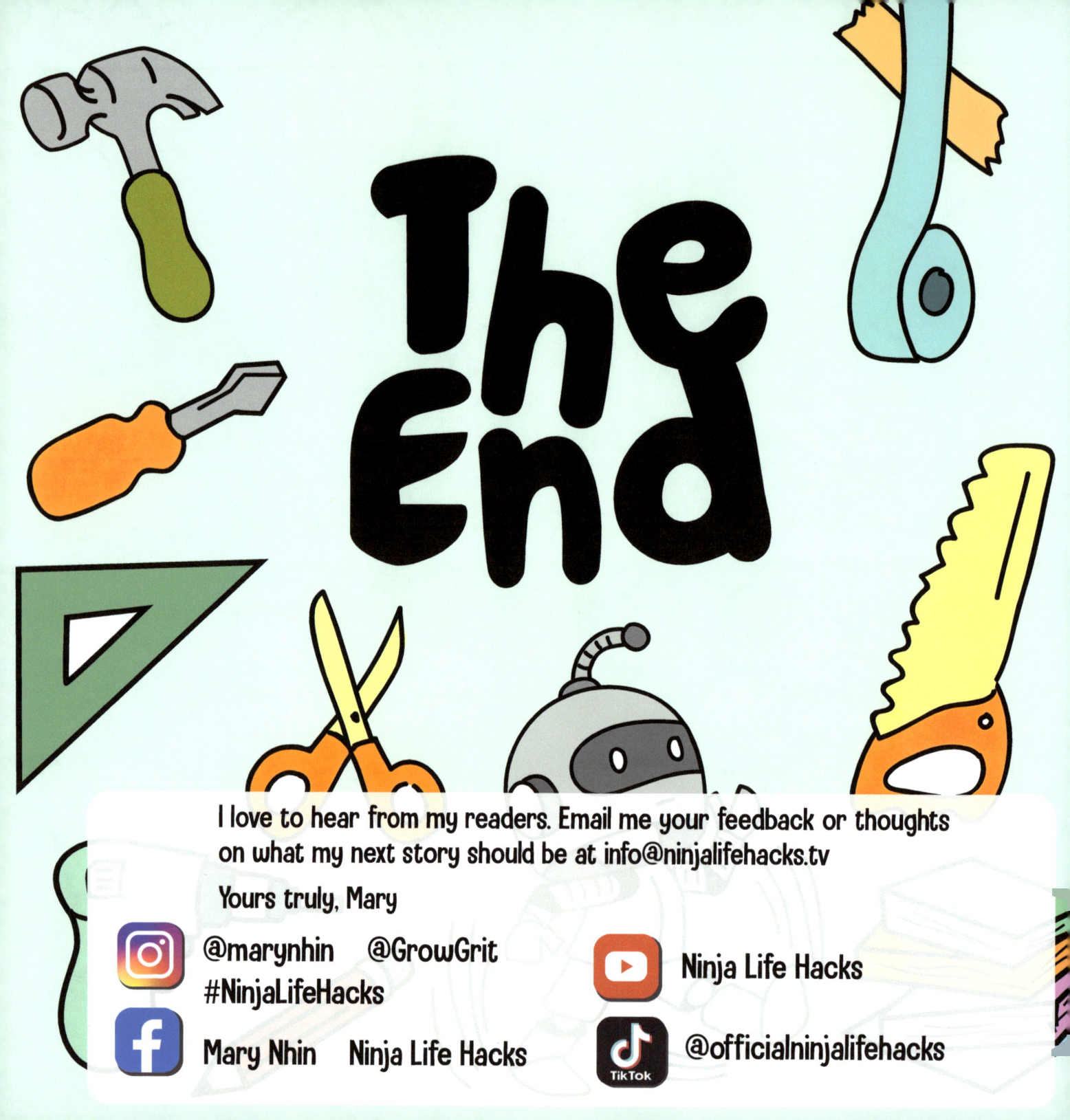

# The End

I love to hear from my readers. Email me your feedback or thoughts on what my next story should be at info@ninjalifehacks.tv

Yours truly, Mary

@marynhin  @GrowGrit
#NinjaLifeHacks

Mary Nhin  Ninja Life Hacks

Ninja Life Hacks

@officialninjalifehacks

Continue the learning with fun social, emotional worksheets and printables at ninjalifehacks.tv

# ROBOT STEM ACTIVITY

**Challenge**: Create a robot. Learn how gravity works as the robot walks by rocking back and forth on its curved feet. As the robot rocks from one foot to the other, gravity pulls the feet down the incline. So it rocks to the right, and the left foot (which is no longer touching the board) moves forward. It rocks to the left, and the right foot moves forward. Pretty rad to watch! If you don't want to cut up the page, this fun activity is also contained in the Engineer Ninja Lesson Plans on ninjalifehacks.tv

## Supplies needed:

- ⊘ Construction paper
- ⊘ Scissors
- ⊘ Incline
- ⊘ Robot template

# Instructions:

1. Print and cut out the template.
2. Fold along the dotted lines.
3. Curl the tail with a pen.
4. Fold your head in any which way you'd like.
5. Place on an incline and watch your robot walk.

# Hints for discovery:
The surface that the robot walks on is key. It needs to have enough friction, but not too much. The angles are also important. The legs' angles make the dog rock side to side, and gravity pulls the robot down the ramp.

# Troubleshooting tips:

- If your robot is having trouble walking, what could you change?
- Does the friction incline of your ramp need to change?
- Does the head or tail need to change direction?
- Does the angle of the legs need to change?
- Do you need to cut a little more angle on the feet?

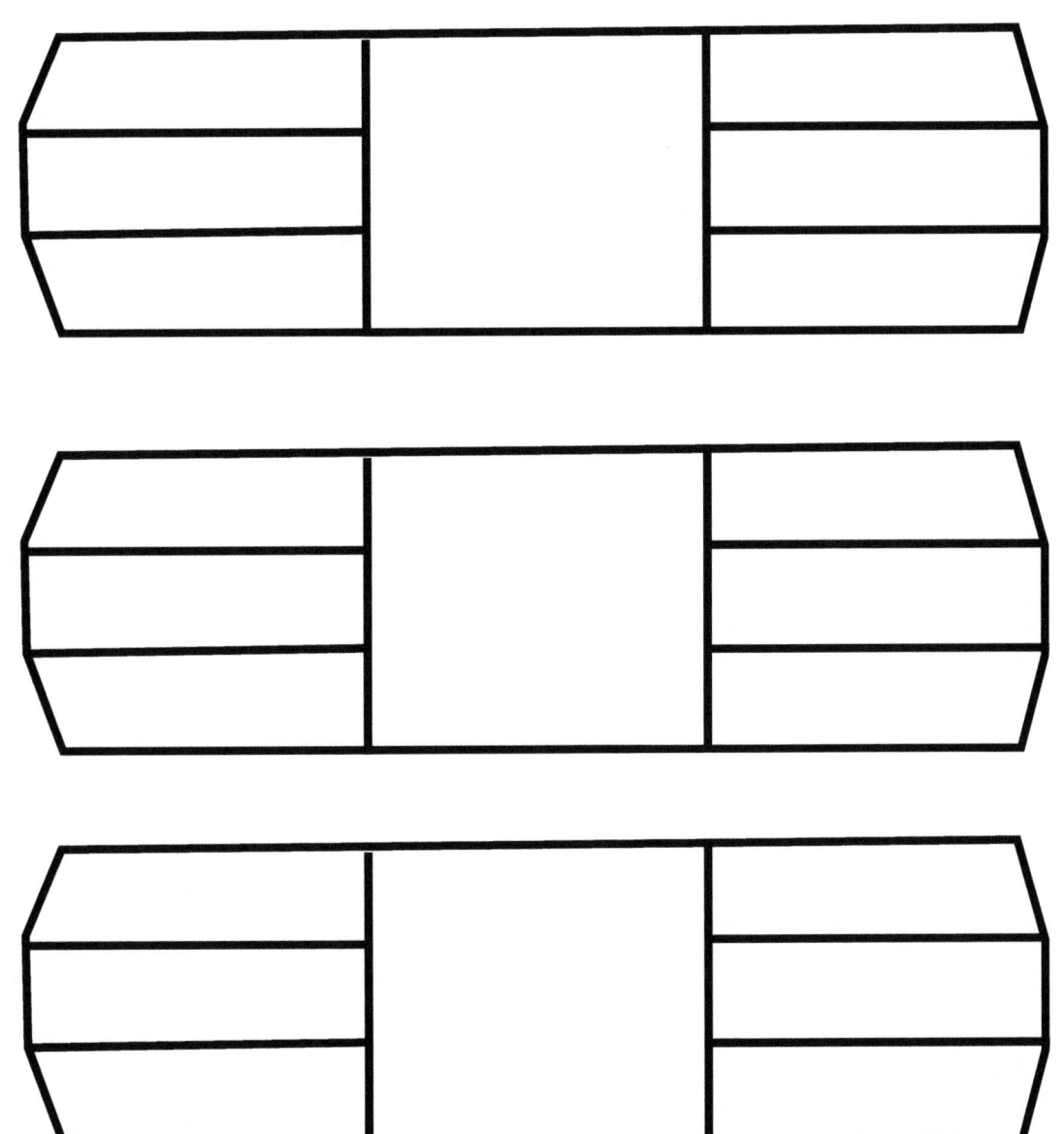

www.ingramcontent.com/pod-product-compliance
Lightning Source LLC
Chambersburg PA
CBHW041713160426
43209CB00018B/1824